The Unicorn and the Brave Princess

Written by Claire Philip Illustrated by Megan Higgins

Miles Kelly

In a land far away, there lived
a princess called Scarlett.

She spent her days
exploring and longing for
adventure!

The princess didn't want to skip and play with the other girls.

She wanted to climb trees, swim in rivers, and find trolls instead.

As Scarlett did her homework each day, she daydreamed about taming a dragon.

And as she did her chores, she imagined climbing a tall tower to rescue a prince.

Help!

Scarlett's parents thought
that she was a little too wild.

"All she wants to do
is have adventures!"
said the queen.

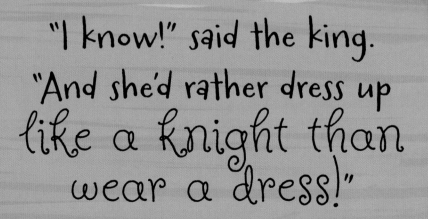

"I know!" said the king.
"And she'd rather dress up
like a knight than
wear a dress!"

Scarlett overheard
their conversation
and felt a little sad.

'Why am I
different?'
she wondered.

"I'll have one more of day of fun," said Scarlett, "and then I'll be a proper princess."

The next day Scarlett wore a dress, but she didn't really like it.

"You look so sweet!" said the queen.

Instead of going to play outside, the princess baked cupcakes. They tasted nice, but she was quite bored.

'I wish I was in the forest,' Scarlett thought.

Later that day, Scarlett went for a walk. Suddenly she saw a flash of white, and there before her was a UNICORN!

"Wow!" said Scarlett. The unicorn was very beautiful.

It sparkled in the sunshine!

Scarlett
stroked the
unicorn.

"I need your help,
princess," it said.
"My friend, a prince, has
been locked in a tower.

A dragon is guarding the way.
Will you help me RESCUE him?"

Scarlett smiled, "I'd love to help!" and she jumped on the unicorn's back.

Quick as a flash they set
off into the forest.

Scarlett laughed with joy as they
whizzed past an angry-looking troll.

Soon, they came across a sleeping dragon. There wasn't much room to pass.

They could see the tower in the distance.

"If I move one of her eggs," whispered Scarlett, "she'll leave the path to save it."

Carefully she moved one, just out of the way, then whistled to wake the dragon.

The dragon heard, and rushed
to collect her egg.

Scarlett and the unicorn
dashed behind her, and ran
to the tower!

"The key to the door is in the knot of the willow tree," called the prince.

Quickly, Scarlett found it, and opened the door.

The prince rushed out and cried,
"Thank you! My stepfather locked
me up to steal my throne!

You saved me. Now
I can return home!"

They walked back
down the path together,
and parted as friends.

The dragon had gone back to sleep,
this time wrapped around her eggs.

Back at the palace, the unicorn said, "Goodbye, princess. I hope to see you again."

And with a huge smile, Scarlett went inside, thinking, 'I chose adventures, after all...'